Pete and Polo
and the
Washday Adventure

Adrian Reynolds

 ORCHARD BOOKS

For my Mum and Dad

A.R.

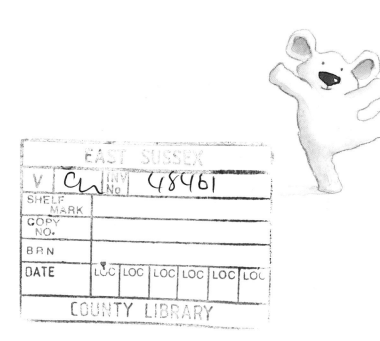

ORCHARD BOOKS
96 Leonard Street, London EC2A 4RH
Orchard Books, Australia
14 Mars Road, Lane Cove, NSW 2066
©Adrian Reynolds 1997
ISBN 1 86039 354 3 (hardback)
ISBN 1 86039 777 8 (paperback)
First published in Great Britain in 1997
First published in paperback in 1998
The right of Adrian Reynolds to be identified as the author and illustrator
of this Work has been asserted by him in accordance with the
Copyright, Designs and Patents Act1998.
A CIP catalogue record of this book is available
from the British Library
Printed in Hong Kong/China

Every day, when breakfast is over,
Pete and Polo set off on an adventure together.

They climb the highest mountains together...

they hide in the deepest darkest caves together...

they explore the most dangerous tiger-infested
jungles together…

and they battle with huge scary monsters.

One afternoon, after escaping from a dangerous monster, Pete and Polo met Mum at the door.

"Oh, Pete," she said. "Just look at the state of Polo. You really should take better care of him."

"I am a bit dirty," said Polo. Pete had to agree.

The next morning Polo
was nowhere to be seen.
"That's strange," said Pete.
"Polo always waits for me."
Where could he be?
Pete went searching for him.

Polo wasn't hiding in the deep dark cave...

he wasn't climbing up the mountain…

Pete searched through the dangerous jungle
but Polo wasn't there either.

Pete was afraid that Polo had been gobbled up
by the huge scary monster.

Pete began to search the whole house.
He looked under the stairs…

he looked on top of shelves…

he looked under the beds…

he looked behind the curtains...

and he even looked in the rubbish bin...

but Polo was nowhere to be found.

By this time Pete was feeling very
sad and lonely and a little bit sniffy.

Suddenly Mum appeared, and there was Polo! He looked all clean and white.

"Look, Pete," he said. "I'm not dirty any more. I've been having an adventure all by myself. I've been swimming in deep bubbly seas."

Pete wanted to give Polo
a great big hug.

"Wait," cried Polo. "Look at
the state you're in. You can't
hug me until you're clean.
It's your turn to go swimming."

And Pete had to agree.

Pete and Polo both agreed that
swimming in deep bubbly seas
was quite an adventure too.